The Patchwork Path

A QUILT MAP TO FREEDOM

Bettye Stroud

illustrated by

Erin Susanne Bennett

CANDLEWICK PRESS

CAMBRIDGE, MASSACHUSETTS

My name is Hannah. I was a slave on a Georgia plantation.

The year I turned ten, Mama taught me to make a special quilt. I learned how to stitch together pieces of old cloth to make different patterns. But Mama wanted me to learn more than just how to sew. While we stitched, she told me a secret.

"Each pattern holds a special meaning," Mama whispered. "Hannah, this quilt will show you everything you need to know to run to freedom."

She and Papa thought about freedom all the time. I dared to think about it, too, after Mama taught me about the quilt patterns.

Soon after Master sold my sister, Mary, to a far-off plantation, Mama passed away. Papa said it was her heart that broke. Sometimes, when I missed Mama and Mary so hard and my own heart was close to splitting, I remembered Mama's words:

 The *monkey wrench*

 turns the *wagon wheel*

 toward Canada on a *bear's paw* trail

to the crossroads.

 Once they got to the *crossroads,*

 they dug a *log cabin* on the ground.

 Shoofly told them to dress up in cotton

 and satin *bow ties* and go to

the cathedral church, get married,

and exchange double rings.

 *Flying geese* stay on

the *drunkard's path* and

 follow the *stars.*

That was the quilt code.

 *One day in spring,* Papa told me to air out Mama's Monkey Wrench quilt.

"This pattern warns the others that you and I are leaving, that we are gathering our tools to go. It will be a long and difficult journey. But remember, Mama is up in heaven, watching over us. Tomorrow night, storms will come, and we'll run. So get your quilt. Tie the corners together and slip a little bread inside."

I shook with excitement but wished Mary were with us. I wondered what it was like where she lived now, and if at night she looked up at the sky toward Mama.

Papa was a wagon driver.
When he drove the mules to other plantations, he kept his eyes open, going and coming, for miles and miles around. He memorized roads, streams, and dark woods. Papa knew where runaway slaves could hide.

The night before we left, Papa tried to calm me. I touched a finger to the wagon-wheel square on my quilt. I knew it meant we were to pack things for the journey, as though we were loading a wagon. I also knew there would be no wagon, that we would have to run.

We stepped out into the worst rainstorm
I'd ever seen. "Papa, do we have to leave now?"
I asked.

"Yes. The dogs won't be able to follow our scent. No work
in the fields tomorrow, so Master won't miss us."

In the drenching rain, he led me through the dark woods. Did
I hear the hooves of galloping horses? We hid behind fallen logs.
I shivered from the wet cold. I thought I heard a dog bark, and a stick
snap. My stomach tightened. Would they catch us and take us back?
What would happen to us then?

Early the next morning, we came to a church at the edge of town. "With a storm like this, the members here will be expecting runaway slaves," Papa said. We crept inside.

We hid in a secret place beneath the floor. Daylight slanted through holes cut into the wooden planks. "That cross shape is from Africa," Papa told me. "It means life, death, and rebirth."

I prayed then that we would be reborn as free people in Canada. The soft voices of our protectors drifted down to us as we waited for nightfall.

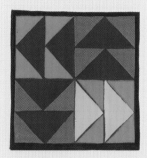 *Papa's lantern* cast strange shadows on the walls of the tunnel that led from the church to the river. Papa told me that pirates had made the tunnels.

We followed the riverbed upstream. The cold water soaked my shoes. My toes felt like icy, hard pebbles. Sometimes Papa climbed the bluff to look for horsemen with dogs and whips.

My knees and legs ached. How far was Canada anyway?

Just as the sun rose, I saw a flock of geese high above. "They're flying North," said Papa. "We'll follow them."

 *We walked* night after night and hid during the day. When I felt I couldn't lift my legs, I thought about Mama and her quilt code. She kept me going.

I had never left the plantation or seen anything but fields and marsh. I could not believe my eyes when we climbed high into the mountains and saw the view! Surely we could see Canada from there, but Papa shook his head. "No, Hannah, we're still far off. We need to find a way down this mountain."

A little farther on, I found the way. "Look, Papa, there it is! There are the bear tracks—like on my quilt."

We followed the bear's paw trail to the valley below. I hoped we wouldn't catch up to the bears. The tracks led us to water and an empty, safe cave to sleep in. Mama's quilt patterns worked just fine.

*Sometimes* we had something to eat, and sometimes we went hungry. We considered ourselves lucky when there were berries to pick. Bees stung me when I tried to get honey from a hive. If Papa caught a fish from a stream, we enjoyed a feast!

Spring turned to summer, and now even the nights were warm. We kept walking in a zigzag pattern, like the drunkard's path on my quilt. I remembered Mama had told me once that bad luck follows a straight line. I knew the zigzag pattern would make it harder for Master's men to follow our trail, too.

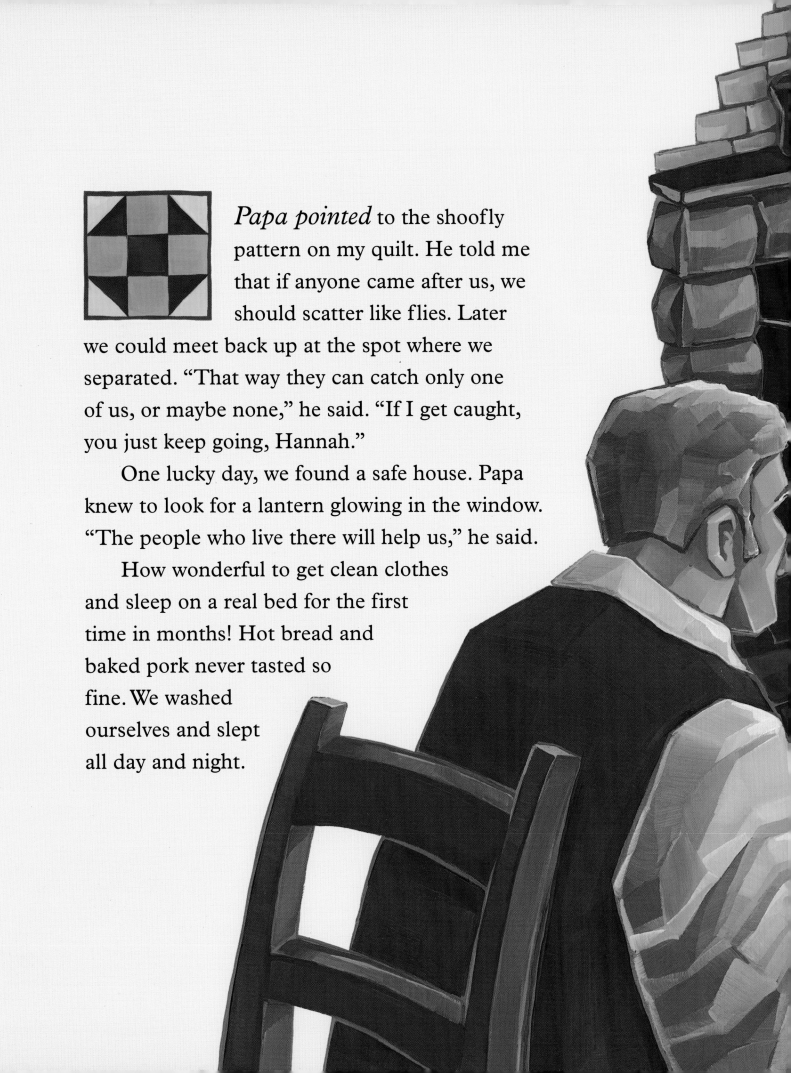

Papa pointed to the shoofly pattern on my quilt. He told me that if anyone came after us, we should scatter like flies. Later we could meet back up at the spot where we separated. "That way they can catch only one of us, or maybe none," he said. "If I get caught, you just keep going, Hannah."

One lucky day, we found a safe house. Papa knew to look for a lantern glowing in the window. "The people who live there will help us," he said.

How wonderful to get clean clothes and sleep on a real bed for the first time in months! Hot bread and baked pork never tasted so fine. We washed ourselves and slept all day and night.

Next morning, the good man
and his wife told us they were
Quakers. They believed that
slavery was wrong and said they
would help us as much as they could. Next they
told us what lay ahead on our way to a place called
Cleveland, to the crossroads. I listened close.

Two days later, the man carried us northward
for miles as we lay hidden in the bottom of his
wagon, covered by blankets and straw.

When night fell, we struck out walking again.
I felt rested and ready to go get freedom. But
freedom was still a far way off.

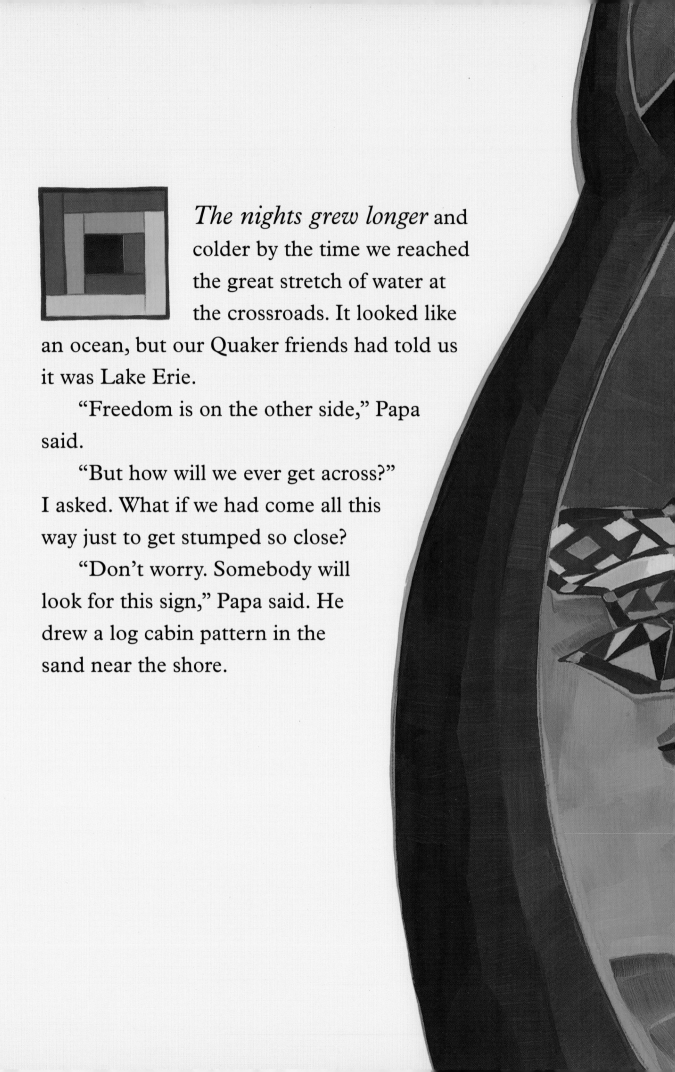

The nights grew longer and colder by the time we reached the great stretch of water at the crossroads. It looked like an ocean, but our Quaker friends had told us it was Lake Erie.

"Freedom is on the other side," Papa said.

"But how will we ever get across?" I asked. What if we had come all this way just to get stumped so close?

"Don't worry. Somebody will look for this sign," Papa said. He drew a log cabin pattern in the sand near the shore.

 *We hid* in a nearby graveyard and waited. A free black man saw our sign and looked around for us. We rushed out of hiding, and the man took us to a big cave that looked like a cathedral. He gave us clean clothes. I got a crisp new bonnet to wear. As Papa tied the strings into a big bow, I thought, "The bow-tie square on my quilt!" We dressed up like we were going to church.

With our new clothes, we looked like we were free. The man told us, "You've always been free on the inside. Now your old life is over. Soon you'll be free on the outside, too."

That night, Papa rang a small bell that the man had given him. We waited for a signal, a sign. We heard a faint chime as somebody rang back. Double rings!

A riverboat captain took us on his boat, and we set out across the water. The North Star shone brightly in the night sky. We had followed the stars to freedom.

As dawn spread pink across the water, I saw Canada. It was autumn now, and the trees, with their red and gold leaves, looked like they were on fire. What a beautiful place! We felt truly reborn. I hugged Papa tight.

I spent our first winter making a new quilt, using pieces of cloth from our old slave clothes and some new fabric, too. A big one this time, with all the patterns of the quilt code, just like Mama had taught me. I left one square empty because I missed my sister.

When Mary is with us again, I'll finish the quilt. Until then, I'll pray for her and dream about all of us being free.

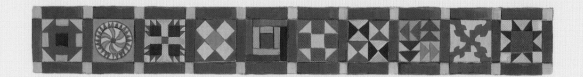

AFTERWORD

The Patchwork Path is based on a story given to Jacqueline Tobin by African-American quilter Ozella McDaniel Williams at the historic Charleston, South Carolina, marketplace in 1994. The story, about how slaves used quilts to communicate on the Underground Railroad, had been passed down orally from grandmother to mother to daughter. The story was held secret in Ozella's family until she insisted that Jacqueline "write this down."

In 1999, Jacqueline Tobin and Dr. Raymond Dobard published *Hidden in Plain View: A Secret Story of Quilts and the Underground Railroad.* Since then, Ozella's story has inspired thousands to listen to the stories of their elders and pass them on.

The church in this story really exists. The First African Baptist Church in Savannah, Georgia, is the oldest black church in North America. Built by slaves who were allowed to build only after their day's work ended, the church served as a stop on the Underground Railroad. The cross pattern Papa points out to Hannah, which is called a Congolese cosmogram, can still be seen on the floorboards of the auditorium.

It is also true that pirates made the tunnels that Hannah and Papa walk through. When the slaves built the church, they secretly connected the church basement to a tunnel, knowing it would serve as a useful escape route.

This book is testament to the ingenuity and creativity of the many slaves who risked everything to gain their freedom.

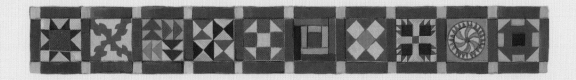

To Kesha, with love
B. S.

To Timothy, my inspiration
E. S. B.

The author wishes to thank Jacqueline Tobin and Raymond Dobard
for their help on this book, and for the use of the quilt code written about in
Hidden in Plain View (Doubleday, 1999).

Design Press wishes to thank Reverend Thurmond Tillman, Pastor of
First African Baptist Church of Savannah, Georgia, for his help.

Text copyright © 2005 by Bettye Stroud
Illustrations copyright © 2005 by Erin Susanne Bennett

Design Press is a division of the Savannah College of Art and Design.

First paperback edition 2007

The Library of Congress has cataloged the hardcover edition as follows:
Stroud, Bettye, date.
The patchwork path: a quilt map to freedom / Bettye Stroud ; illustrated
by Erin Susanne Bennett. — 1st ed.
p.   cm.
Summary: While her father leads her toward Canada and away from the plantation
where they have been slaves, a young girl thinks of the quilt her mother used to teach
her a code that will help guide them to freedom.
ISBN 978-0-7636-2423-1 (hardcover)
[1. Fugitive slaves — Fiction. 2. Quilts — Fiction. 3. Underground railroad — Fiction.
4. Slavery — Fiction. 5. African Americans — Fiction.]   I. Bennett, Erin Susanne, ill.
II. Title
PZ7.S92473Pat 2005
[E] — dc22   2004045786

ISBN 978-0-7636-3519-0 (paperback)

2 4 6 8 10 9 7 5 3

Printed in China

This book was typeset in Plantin.
The illustrations were done in oil.

Candlewick Press
2067 Massachusetts Avenue
Cambridge, Massachusetts 02140

visit us at www.candlewick.com